This Little Tiger book belongs to.

_____

_____

_____

_____

For Sue and Paul
A.H.B.

For Jess
T.W.

LITTLE TIGER PRESS
An imprint of Magi Publications
1 The Coda Centre, 189 Munster Road, London SW6 6AW
www.littletigerpress.com
First published in Great Britain 1998
This edition published 2004
Text copyright © A.H. Benjamin 1998
Illustrations copyright © Tim Warnes 1998
A.H. Benjamin and Tim Warnes have asserted their rights to
be identified as the author and illustrator of this work under
the Copyright, Designs and Patents Act, 1988
A CIP catalogue record for this book is available from the
British Library
All rights reserved • ISBN 1 84506 066 0
Printed in China
10 9 8 7 6 5 4 3 2

# IT COULD HAVE BEEN WORSE...

by **A.H. Benjamin**
illustrated by **Tim Warnes**

Mouse was on his way back home
after visiting his town cousin,
when . . .

WHOOPS!

...he lost his balance
and fell to the ground.

"Ouch!" said Mouse. "This isn't my lucky day."

But it could have been worse!

Mouse picked himself up
and carried on his way.
He came to an open field
and was scurrying across it,
when . . .

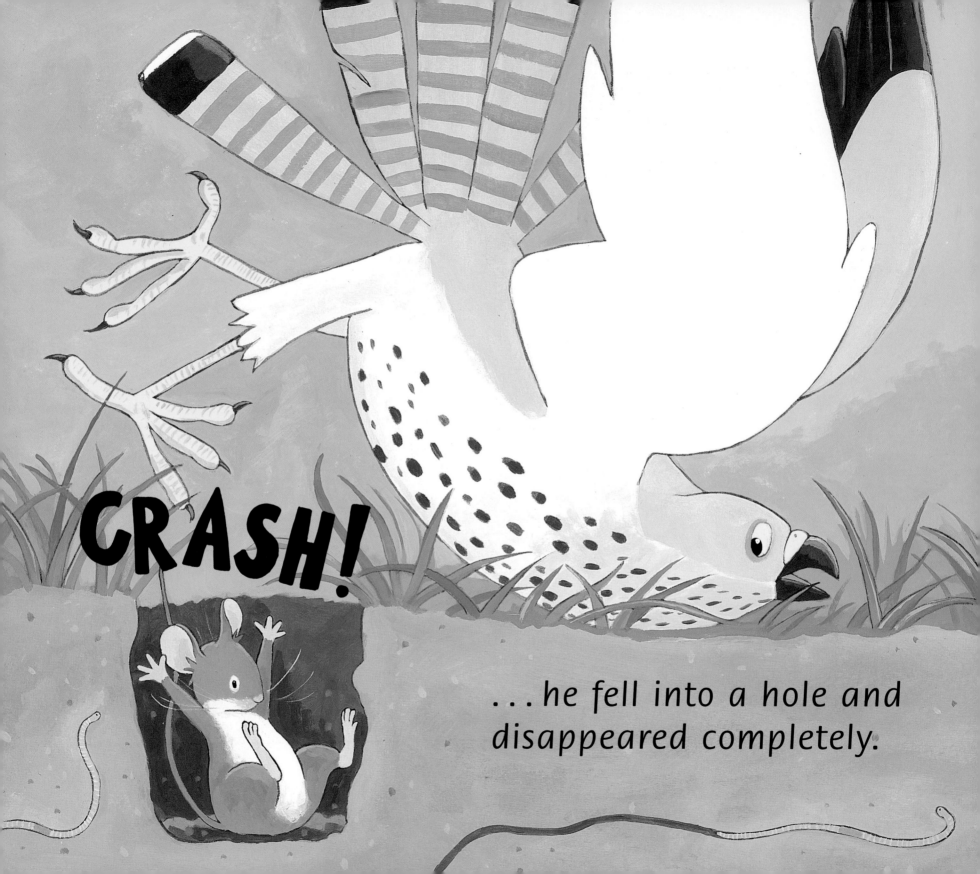

CRASH!

...he fell into a hole and disappeared completely.

"Why do things *always* go wrong for me?" grumbled Mouse.

But it could have been worse!

Mouse clambered out of the
hole and was off again.

"I think I'll take a rest," he said.
Mouse had just found a nice comfy spot,
when . . .

**OUCH!**

...he sat on a thistle
and shot into the air.

"Everything happens to me!" wailed Mouse as he pulled some prickles out of his bottom.

But it could have been worse!

Mouse walked down the hill until he reached a stream. He began to cross it by stepping on the stones, when . . .

"I'll catch my death of cold!"
complained Mouse.

But it could have been worse!

Mouse paddled to the edge of the
stream and climbed out of the water.

Shaking himself dry, he was just about to scramble down a steep bank, when . . .

**WHEEE!**

...he lost his footing and skidded
right to the bottom.

"I'll be black and blue all over," cried Mouse.

But it could have been worse!

Mouse staggered to his feet
and ran all the way home.

"It's been a terrible day," he said to his mum
as she bathed his cuts and bruises. "I fell into
a hole, got wet in the river and –"
"Never mind, Son," said Mum . . .

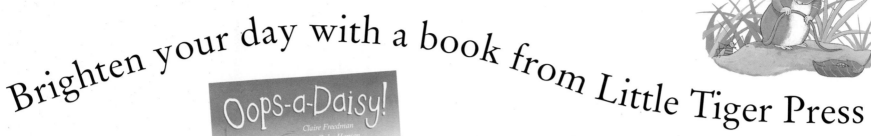

Brighten your day with a book from Little Tiger Press

Oops-a-Daisy!
Claire Freedman
Gaby Hansen

Who's Been Eating My Porridge?
M Christina Butler
Daniel Howarth

QUIET!
Paul Bright
illustrated by
Guy Parker-Rees

Fidgety Fish
Ruth Galloway

Love Like This
PETER KAVANAGH & JANE CHAPMAN

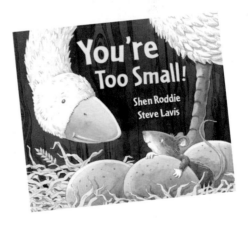

You're Too Small!
Shen Roddie
Steve Lavis

For information regarding any of the above titles or
for our catalogue, please contact us: Little Tiger Press,
1 The Coda Centre, 189 Munster Road, London SW6 6AW
Tel: 020 7385 6333  Fax: 020 7385 7333
Email: info@littletiger.co.uk  www.littletigerpress.com